ISBN 0-9627301-0-6

Published by:
Grand Hotel
Mackinac Island
Michigan 49757

Rebecca of Grand Hotel
by Robin E. M. Agnew

Hi, my name is Rebecca.
I live at Grand Hotel
on Mackinac Island
with Beaumont, my dog.

Beaumont and I have
our own table in the
dining room, and our
favorite waiter, Chester.

Here's how I spend my time —
shopping,

having picnics with Chester,

swimming in rocky,
freezing Lake Huron,

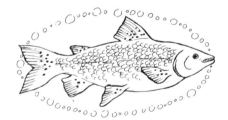

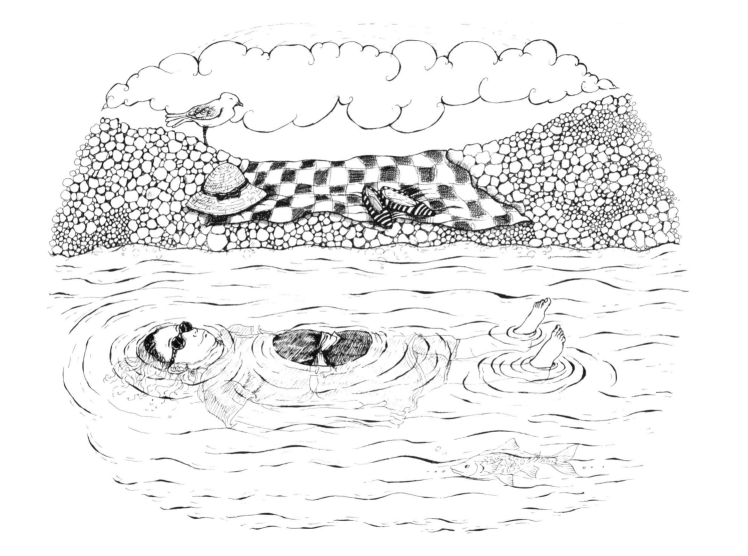

playing tennis — badly —
with the pro,

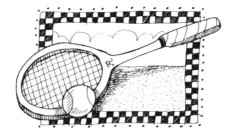

watching the dressed up grown-ups dance
in the Terrace Room at night,

and on lucky days, watching a bellman
catch a stray bat or two,

or going to parades.

Anyway, believe it or not, sometimes even all that stuff gets a little dull. In the winters it's just me, Chester, and Beaumont making sandwiches in the hotel kitchen.

White Footed Mouse

One winter, a wolf walked over to the island across the frozen lake. That was exciting but it didn't last very long.

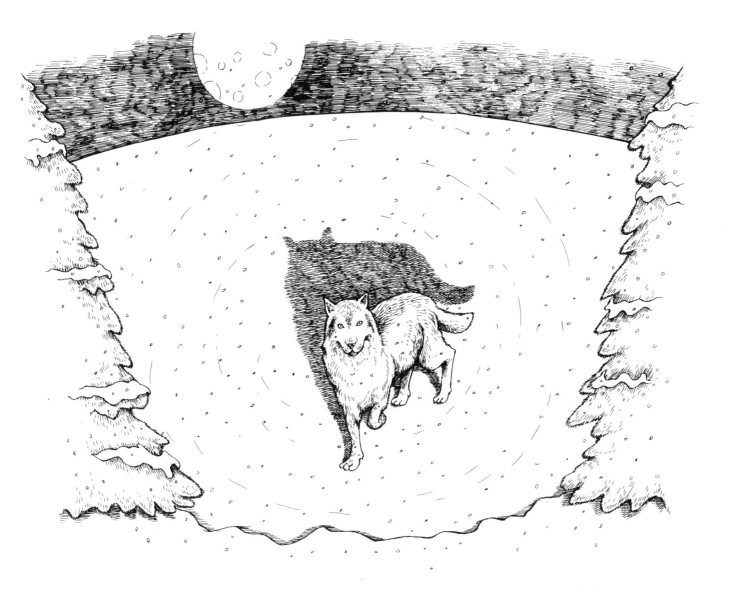

Last summer I started spending time on the golf
course. It was fun watching the golfers, and
the golf course was a good short cut to Fort Mackinac.

One day I was over on the golf course and I saw this bicycle. I don't know what it was, but there was something really great about that bike. So, the next morning, Chester packed me a picnic and I climbed on the bicycle. Except for swimming and parades, I really didn't know that much about the island and wanted to see some more of it.

That bike seemed to take me so fast.
I couldn't stop. I even rode through
the lilac parade and ended up with the
Queen's tiara. After riding by the lake awhile,
I saw a path of stepping stones going up into
the woods. I was hungry so I decided to stop there.

I climbed up and up the path and I saw the
smallest house I had ever seen.
It fit in the woods perfectly, so perfectly
it had been impossible to see from the road.

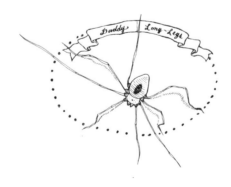

It was the best spot so far for a picnic,
and, since the house looked empty, I sat
down on the porch to have my lunch.

When I had almost finished, I heard a noise.
It wasn't really a scary noise, it was a forest
noise, so I began to look around. What I saw
was a boy who fit into the woods as perfectly
as the house, and who had been almost impossible to see.
"Hello," said the boy. "My name is William.
I sent my bicycle for you."
"Hello," I said, "My name is Rebecca."
"I know who you are,"said William.
"I sent my bicycle because I thought
it was time you learned something about the island."
So off we went.

When I went places with William, I saw things I never saw with anyone else. That first day he took me to pretty ordinary places, but they all seemed much more than ordinary to me.

First, we went to William's favorite wild strawberry patch. I had no idea that you could pick free strawberries in the woods, and that they would taste so good. We both ate so many that we had to take a rest.

Then William showed me the crack-in-the-island. He poked a stick in it and — well, you can see what happened. We didn't stay there very long.

Next, we went to Fort Holmes, which is on even higher ground than Fort Mackinac. From Fort Holmes you can see everything. William told me that if we sat very still we could see Indian spirits, but I didn't see a thing.

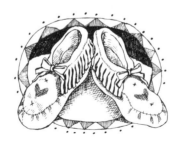

William also took me to Brown's Brook. He said
he thought I would like to see all the wild flowers
that grew there. I'd never seen so many animals.
When I've gone by myself it's never been as crowded
as it was that day.

Then we went to Devils Kitchen, which is just an old limestone cave on the lake. We climbed way up on top. William said the mouth of the cave was really the ghost of a dead giant. It was a neat cave, but we didn't see any ghosts there either.

At the end of our day, William gave me a ride
on his bicycle back to the hotel. I invited
him to come for dinner sometime.

William came to dinner the very next day, and we had an extra fun time.

At the end of that summer, I felt so sad.
I thought William would leave like everyone
else did, and it would be just me, Chester,
and Beaumont again, all winter.

Just as I was thinking about him, William appeared. "Here, Rebecca," he said. "I want you to have this." And he dropped a locket into my hand. When I looked up again, he was gone. "Thank you, William," I said to thin air. I felt extra sad.

Well, as the snow started to fall again, and as the lake began to freeze, Chester told me he had some news. He said it was time for me to start going to school. Can you guess who was in my very first class in school?

My winters are just as interesting as my summers now. William even invites Beaumont and me over for dinner, and he's teaching me how to cook!

I hope all of you who have read my story will have as much fun on Mackinac as I did. If you look around the hotel and see what you can see, you may even find a picture of someone that you know, with a certain locket on.